Camping
Catastrophe!

by ABBY KLEIN

illustrated by
JOHN MCKINLEY

THE BLUE SKY PRESS
An Imprint of Scholastic Inc. • New York

To J. C.
Lover of the outdoors
and the best brother in the world!
A. K.

THE BLUE SKY PRESS

Text copyright © 2008 by Abby Klein
Illustrations copyright © 2008 by John McKinley
All rights reserved.

Special thanks to Robert Martin Staenberg.

No part of this publication may be reproduced, stored in
a retrieval system, or transmitted in any form or by any means,
electronic, mechanical, photocopying, recording, or otherwise,
without written permission of the publisher. For information
regarding permission, please write to: Permissions Department,
Scholastic Inc., 557 Broadway, New York, New York 10012.
SCHOLASTIC, THE BLUE SKY PRESS, and associated logos are
trademarks and/or registered trademarks of Scholastic Inc.
Library of Congress catalog card number: 2007036387
ISBN-13: 978-0-439-89594-1 / ISBN-10: 0-439-89594-4
18 17   12 13
Printed in the United States of America 40
First printing, August 2008

CHAPTERS

I have a problem.

A really, really, big problem.

My dad and I are going camping

this weekend, but my dad

doesn't know anything about

the wilderness, and I'm afraid

of the dark. I hope we survive!

Let me tell you about it.

CHAPTER 1

Snakes and Skunks

"I can't wait until tomorrow!" I said to my best friend, Robbie, as we sat eating our lunches.

"Me neither," he said. "It's going to be so much fun!"

"What are you dorks talking about?" barked Max, the biggest bully in the whole first grade. "Are you two starting a new ballet class?"

"I'm going to a new ballet class tomorrow," Chloe chirped. "My mom even bought a fancy pink tutu with silver sequins. . . ."

"No one cares," Max interrupted. "Besides, I

wasn't talking to you. I was talking to Freddy and Robbie."

"Well, you don't have to be so rude," Chloe continued. "I was just saying—"

Max cut her off and turned back to us. "So, what are you two doing that is going to be so much fun? This ought to be good."

"We're going camping with my dad," I said, smiling proudly.

"Where?" said Max, chuckling. "In your backyard?"

"For your information," said Robbie, "we are going to spend the night out in the wilderness."

"Really?" said my friend Jessie. "That sounds so cool. I always wanted to go camping."

"I know. Me, too," I said.

"What kinds of things are you going to do?"

"First, we have to pitch a tent. Then we'll probably go fishing and swimming in the lake. We'll build a campfire and make s'mores."

"Where are you going to sleep?" asked Chloe.

"What do you mean?" said Robbie. "In the tent, of course! In sleeping bags."

"But that's so dirty," Chloe said, wrinkling up her nose. "And there are so many bugs."

"That's the fun of it," said Jessie.

"YUCK! I don't want bugs crawling on me in the middle of the night."

"Yeah, they might even crawl up your nose!" Max said, wiggling his fingers like a spider on Chloe's face.

"EEEEWWWW!" Chloe screamed, slapping Max's hand away. "Get your hands off me. You are so gross."

"And you're such a baby," Max said, laughing.

"I am not!"

"You are, too!"

"Am not," Chloe whined.

"Are, too."

"I'm going to tell Miss Becky on you," Chloe

cried as she got up from the table and stomped off to find the lunch aide, Becky.

"Baby!" Max called after her and stuck his tongue out. Then he turned back to us. "Pitching tents? Fishing? Ha! What do the two of you know about that?"

"Well, I ummmm . . ."

"A big, fat nothing. You two babies don't know anything about camping."

"I bet they know more than you," Jessie interrupted, pointing her finger in Max's face. "I bet you've never slept anywhere but in your own bed with your little teddy weddy bear and your baby blanket."

Boy, when it comes to Max, Jessie is so brave. She is never afraid to stand up to him.

"Well, I uh . . ." Max stammered.

"Exactly, just as I thought," Jessie said. "You've never been camping before, so stop acting like such a big shot."

Max stared at her. He opened his mouth, but nothing came out. He didn't really know what to say.

How does she do that? "Thanks. That was great!" I whispered to Jessie.

"It's nothing." She smiled. "So how long are you guys going to be gone for?"

"We're just going for one night," said Robbie. "Freddy's dad has never been camping before, so we thought one night would be a good way to start."

"You guys are going to have a blast."

"Yeah, my dad said that we are going to catch lots of fish and cook them for dinner. I'm going to catch a really big one."

"Me, too," added Robbie. "I'm going to catch one bigger than your head, Freddy."

"Are you going to tell ghost stories around the campfire?" asked Jessie.

"Of course," Robbie said. "I know some really scary ones."

"Of course we are," I answered, trying to sound brave, but secretly hoping that Robbie's stories wouldn't be too scary. After all, just the sounds of all the night creatures were enough to scare the pants off of me.

"Just watch out for the two s's," said Jessie.

"The two s's?"

"Yeah, the snakes and the skunks."

"Ha-ha," Max laughed. "The skunks. You mean the stink bombs."

"What do you mean, the snakes and the skunks?" I asked nervously.

"Don't you know the woods are full of them?" said Robbie. "It's their natural habitat."

Robbie is a science genius, and he knows a lot about animals, so I knew he wasn't making this up just to freak me out.

"Uh . . . nobody said anything about snakes and skunks."

"Don't worry, they won't bother you if you don't bother them."

"If you say so." I was beginning to wonder if this trip was such a good idea.

"Oh, stop worrying, Freddy. We're going to have a great time!"

"Who said I was worried?"

"It's going to be a real adventure," Jessie said, patting me on the back. "I wish I were going."

"Yeah, it'll be great," I said, smiling weakly. "A real adventure."

CHAPTER 2

The Bet

The next morning I was up, dressed, and was ready to go at the crack of dawn. I ran into my parents' room and jumped on top of my dad while he was sleeping.

"Uuuuffff!" my dad cried. Then with his eyes still closed he mumbled, "Freddy, why are you tackling me in the middle of the night?"

"It's time to get up, Dad. Let's go, go, go!" I said, trying to pull him out of bed. He was as heavy as a bag of rocks.

"What time is it?" he asked, rubbing his eyes and squinting at the clock.

"Morning."

"Freddy, honey," my mom said, yawning, "it's only five o'clock in the morning. Go back to sleep."

"I can't, Mom. Dad and I have to get ready to go camping."

"But you're not leaving for another four hours. Robbie's mom said she'd drop him off at nine o'clock."

"Four hours! I can't wait that long!"

"Well, I'm afraid you're going to have to," my dad grumbled. "And if you don't let me get a little more sleep, then we might not be going at all."

"You don't really mean that. Do you, Dad?"

"Freddy, your father just needs a little more rest. Since you're awake, why don't you go look over the packing list and make sure you haven't forgotten anything."

"Good idea, Mom. I'll be back soon."

"Not too soon," my dad muttered as he rolled over and pulled the covers over his head.

I dashed back to my room and picked up the checklist my mom and I had made, so I would be sure not to forget anything. I ran my finger down the list: sleeping bag, *check*, fishing pole, *check*, canteen, *check*, sharkhead flashlight . . . oh no! My sharkhead flashlight. When I was

packing yesterday, I couldn't find it, and I was going to look for it later, but I forgot. I couldn't go without my sharkhead flashlight. I had to find it!

I looked under my bed first. I found a plastic hammerhead shark, a quarter, and a baseball card I thought I had lost, but no sharkhead flashlight.

I rummaged around in my desk drawer and

pulled out a picture of me and Robbie at the pool, my new sharktooth necklace, and my membership card to the aquarium, but no sharkhead flashlight.

I was starting to get a little panicked. I could not go camping without my sharkhead flashlight. I am afraid of the dark, and I have to sleep with a night-light on. I was secretly planning to leave my sharkhead flashlight on all night inside my sleeping bag.

I sat down on the edge of my bed and hit my forehead with the palm of my hand. "Think, think, think.

"Oh I know," I whispered. "I bet Suzie took it last weekend when she and her friends were having a sleepover, and she never gave it back to me."

I jumped up off the bed and walked across the hall to Suzie's room. Her door was shut, so I turned her doorknob very slowly and tiptoed inside. She was sound asleep and snoring so loudly she sounded like a sick pig. One of these days I was going to have to tape-record her snoring and play it back for her, so she could hear how she sounded. That would be good for a few laughs.

I scanned the room quickly but didn't see the flashlight anywhere. Great! I was going to have to search for it. I got down on my hands and knees and started crawling around her room. I looked on her bookshelf. Not there. I looked on the floor of her closet. Not there. I looked behind her dresser. Not there. I was about to look under her bed when I bumped into the bed by accident.

"AAAAHHHHHH!" Suzie screamed and sat straight up in bed. "Who's there? Who's there?"

I popped up and covered her mouth with my hand. "Shhhhh. It's only me," I whispered.

She yanked my hand off her mouth. "Hey, get your grimy little hand off my mouth! What are you doing in my room in the middle of the night?" she asked angrily.

"It's not the middle of the night."

"Oh whatever. It's still dark outside. The point is, what are you doing in my room without my permission?"

"Looking for something."

"Why are you looking for something of yours in *my* room?"

"Because I think you took it."

"Took what?"

"My sharkhead flashlight."

"Why would I want that stupid thing?"

"Because you needed it when you and your friends were telling ghost stories at your sleepover last weekend."

"No we didn't. Besides, if I needed a flashlight, I would have asked Mom for one. I wouldn't be caught dead with your lame shark one."

"It's not lame."

"Oh yes it is."

"Is not."

"Is, too."

I could see we weren't getting anywhere, and I was leaving in less than a few hours, so I had to find it. "Can you just tell me if you've seen it?" I sighed. "I really need to find it."

"Why do you have to find it so badly?"

"Because I need it for the camping trip."

"I'm sure Robbie will have one the two of you can share."

"I need my own."

"Why?"

"Because."

"Because why?"

"Just because."

"Oh, I think I know why," Suzie said, a smile slowly forming on her lips. "You're afraid of the dark."

"I am not!"

"You are, too! You can't go to sleep without your night-light on. It all makes sense now.

You are planning on using the flashlight like a night-light."

"So?"

"You are such a baby! I bet you don't even make it through the night out there in the wilderness. I bet you guys come home in the middle of the night."

"No we won't."

"Wanna bet?" Suzie asked, holding up her pinkie for a pinkie swear.

"What's the bet?"

"If you come home in the middle of the night, then you have to do my chores for a week, but if you make it through the night, then I have to do yours for a week."

"A week?"

"What's wrong? Afraid you're going to lose the bet?"

"No."

"Then do we have a bet or not? I don't have all day," she said, waving her pinkie at me.

"Fine, the bet's on," I said, and we locked pinkies. "You're going to be really sorry you made it, though, because next week is my week to sweep the garage."

"Oh, I'm not worried," Suzie snickered. "I'm going to love watching you rake up all the leaves."

"Yeah, right," I muttered under my breath.

"You can get out of my room now. I'd like to go back to sleep."

"But I still have to look for my sharkhead flashlight."

"Well, it's not in here," she said, giving me a little shove toward the door.

"Then do you have any idea where it is?"

"I'd love to help you, but I need my beauty sleep. Why don't you look out in the tree house? Maybe you and Robbie took it out there the other day when you were playing detective."

"You're a genius!" I yelled, giving her a great big hug.

"I know. I know. Now can I please go back to sleep?"

"You're the best sister in the whole world!" I called as I ran out of her bedroom, down the stairs, and out the back door.

CHAPTER 3

Tent Trouble

I found my sharkhead flashlight right where Suzie said it might be. Then I waited, and waited, and waited. The morning dragged on. Robbie arrived at exactly nine o'clock. Thank goodness, because I couldn't wait a minute longer! We packed up the car and said good-bye.

My mom squeezed me tight. "Good-bye, honey. You and Robbie are going to have a great time."

"Bye," Suzie said, smiling. "Sleep tight. Don't let the bedbugs bite."

"Oh, we won't," said Robbie. "I brought the bug spray."

"Yeah. See you tomorrow," I said to Suzie. "Ta-ta."

"Or tonight," she whispered in my ear.

I grabbed Robbie by the arm. "Come on. Let's get in the car. I want to get going. Let's not waste any more time here. We've got a lot of things to do today!"

We jumped in the car. My dad said his good-byes, and we were off.

The ride to the campsite seemed to take forever, but we finally got there at about eleven o'clock. Mom had packed sandwiches, and we had just finished them when we arrived.

"Wow! Look at this place," I said as I got out of the car. "It's even cooler than I imagined."

"It's even better than in the pictures," Robbie agreed. "Look at the size of that lake. I bet there's a ton of fish in there."

"What should we do first?" I said, jumping

up and down. "Do you want to go swimming or fishing?"

"Wait just a minute there, guys," my dad interrupted. "We need to do a little work before we play."

"Awwww."

"First things first. We have to set up the tent while it's still daylight. A good camper never waits until nighttime to set up the tent. Let me get it out of the car."

"Wait till you see the tent," I said to Robbie. "It's brand-new. We got it just for this trip."

"Really?"

"Uh-huh. It's huge. It has enough space for four people to sleep, plus it has two zipper doors, and an extra waterproof cover."

"That cover must keep the condensation from collecting on your sleeping bag."

"Uh, English please, Einstein."

"The cover stops the morning dew from soaking your sleeping bag."

"Well, why didn't you just say that?" I said, slapping him on the back.

My dad came back with the tent and set the bag on the ground. "Okeydokey, boys, let's get all of the tent pieces out of the bag before we get started, so we can see what we've got."

"Boy, there sure are a lot of pieces," I said.

"That's what directions are for," said my dad. "You always have to read the directions first before you put anything together."

"My dad tells me the same thing," Robbie whispered to me.

"Freddy, could you please hand me the directions?"

"Sure thing, Dad." I looked in the pile of tent pieces, but I didn't see any directions. "What do the directions look like, Dad?"

"What do you mean what do they look like? What kind of silly question is that? They look like paper with writing on it."

"I don't see any paper here. Just a bunch of poles and stuff."

"It's a small piece of paper with some pictures and some writing on it. I had it out last night. . . ." My dad's voice trailed off.

"Dad?"

"Oh no!"

"What?"

"I took the directions out last night to look at them, and I think I forgot to put them back in the bag."

"Are you kidding me, Dad?"

"I wish I were."

"That's okay, Mr. Thresher," said Robbie. "I bet the three of us can figure out how all of this goes together."

"Yeah, Dad. How hard can it be?"

"I like your attitude, boys."

"I bet we can have this tent put together in a jiffy."

An hour later we were still standing in a mess of tent pieces on the ground. "I give up. This is harder than it looks." I let out a big sigh and plopped myself down on the ground.

"You're not kidding," my dad agreed.

"We've already wasted a lot of time trying to put this dumb tent together. We're not going to get to do any fishing or swimming."

"But if we don't put it together, where are we going to sleep tonight?" my dad asked.

We had better think of something fast. I was not going to lose my bet with Suzie because we couldn't put the tent together.

"I have an idea," Robbie piped up.

Robbie usually had really good ideas. "You do? What?"

"Why don't we just lay the tent on the ground like a tarp and sleep on top of it?"

"That's a great idea!" I said. "You are so smart."

"Good thinking, Robbie," said my dad. "We can sleep out under the stars."

"That sounds even cooler than sleeping in a silly tent."

"I bet you can see a lot of stars out here,"

said Robbie, looking up at the sky. "The skies are probably really clear out here without all the city lights. We can do some stargazing. I know a lot of the constellations. I can teach them to you."

"Awesome! I always wanted to do that."

"Then it's settled," said my dad. "We'll just sleep on top of the tent."

"So, can we go fishing now?"

"Wait, there's one more thing we have to do first."

"Now what?"

"We have to gather some small sticks and pieces of wood for our campfire tonight. If we don't have a fire, then we can't cook the fish we catch."

"Or our s'mores!" I added, licking my lips.

"Why don't you and Robbie take a little walk that way," my dad said, pointing toward the lake, "and I'll go this way. Try to bring back as much firewood as you can carry."

"OK, Dad. We'll meet you right back here in a little bit."

"Just watch where you're walking, boys, and don't stick your hands into any holes," he cautioned us.

"We won't!" we yelled as we started to run off down the path.

"And don't bring any critters back with you!"

40

CHAPTER 4

Buzz, Buzz

Robbie and I walked along the hiking trail, picking up small sticks as we went.

"Hey, look over there," I said, pointing to a small pile of sticks near some rocks. "It looks like someone else was gathering wood but didn't use it all. I'm going over there to get it."

"Hang on there, Freddy," Robbie said, grabbing me by the shirt. "I wouldn't do that if I were you."

"Why not?"

"Remember what Jessie said about snakes and skunks."

"Yeah, so?"

"Well, I don't think a person was collecting those sticks."

"You don't?"

"Nope. That looks like a skunk's den over there. I think a skunk was gathering sticks for his house."

"Really? How do you know?"

"I don't know for sure, but I was doing some research on the computer before we left, and that looks just like the picture of the skunk's den I saw on the Internet."

"Well then, I will definitely stay far away from that," I said, holding my nose and backing away. "I don't want to take any chances of getting sprayed by a skunk."

"I know what you mean," Robbie said, laughing. "Skunks really stink!"

"They are P.U.! Let's get out of here."

We started back down the path, but then all of a sudden, Robbie stopped dead in his tracks. "Shhh," he whispered, and he put up his hand to stop me from walking any farther. "Look over there," he said, pointing to a big rock.

"What?"

"Shhhhh. Over there." He pointed again.

"Where?"

"On that big rock. There's a lizard."

This time when I looked, I saw what he was pointing at. "Wow! I think that's the biggest lizard I've ever seen!"

"I know. His tail must be six inches long!"

"Let's try to catch it."

"But your dad said we weren't allowed to catch any critters."

"He just said we couldn't bring any back with us. He never said we couldn't play with it here," I whispered. I quietly put down the sticks I had been carrying and slowly started to tiptoe toward the lizard.

Robbie followed right behind me. "You go

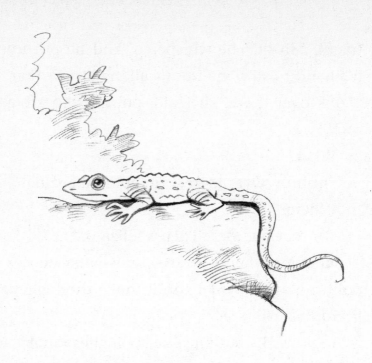

that way, and I'll go this way," I said. "We'll try to surround him so he can't get away."

We tiptoed closer until we were just inches away from catching the lizard. "OK," I mouthed to Robbie, "on the count of three, we grab him." I silently put up one finger at a time. *One, two, three!*

We both pounced on the lizard and could

feel his scaly skin beneath our fingers. "I think we got him! I think we got him!" I yelled. But before we could close our hands around him, he slipped through our fingers and disappeared into the bushes.

"Shoot!" I cried. "We were so close. We almost had him."

"I know," said Robbie. "I thought we had

him, too. Boy, was he fast. He was there one minute and gone the next."

"Bummer. I really wanted to keep him as a pet just for the day since my mom would never let me have anything like that in the house."

"Maybe we can find another one later. We'd better finish collecting the firewood, or your dad's going to wonder what happened to us."

"You're right, and we want to make sure we have enough time for fishing, so we'd better get going."

We both picked up our little piles of sticks and continued on down the path, collecting more sticks as we went. We were almost done when Robbie stopped in front of a big tree.

"Why did you stop?" I asked.

"I'm just looking at something," he said, staring up into the branches.

"What?"

"I think that's a beehive up there," he said, pointing to a branch not far from the ground.

"You think so? A real, live beehive?"

"Yep."

"Do you think there are any bees in there?"

"I don't know. Maybe."

I jumped up and tried to grab hold of the branch, so I could pull it down closer to me.

"Hey, Freddy. What do you think you're doing?"

"I'm just trying to get a closer look. I've never seen a real beehive up close before. I've only seen pictures of them in books."

"And I think you should leave it that way. Do you remember what happened the last time you tried hanging from a tree branch?"

"What?"

"You ended up in the emergency room with a broken arm, that's what!"

"Now you sound like my mom. I'm not going to break my arm," I said, still trying to jump high enough to grab the branch.

"Besides," Robbie continued, "bees don't like it when you disturb their hive."

"Got it!" I said, ignoring Robbie and finally

grabbing hold of the branch. I started to pull the branch down toward the ground to get a closer look when . . . *SNAP!* The branch broke, and the hive hit the ground.

The jolt must have awakened the bees. At first we heard a low buzzing sound, but then all of a sudden the buzzing got louder and louder.

Then a gazillion angry bees burst out of the hive and headed right toward us.

"Run for your life!" Robbie shouted. "It's a swarm, and they're after us!"

"AAAAAHHHHH!" we both screamed as we took off running down the trail with the swarm of angry bees close behind.

CHAPTER 5

Here Fishy, Fishy

"Jump in the lake! Jump in the lake!" Robbie yelled. "The bees can't get us in there!"

We both dove into the lake with all of our clothes on and stayed underwater for a few seconds, hoping the bees would fly away.

When we finally came up for air, the bees had disappeared.

"Phew. That was a close one," I said to Robbie.

"Yeah. A little too close. Next time, would

you please listen to me? I know a lot more about animals than you do."

"From now on, you're the boss," I said.

Just then my dad came down the path. "I thought I heard you two screaming. Is everything all right? And why are you in the lake? I thought I told you boys to collect firewood before you went swimming."

We came out of the lake with our shoes sloshing and our clothes dripping wet.

My dad stared at us for a minute. Then he said, "Would one of you like to tell me what's going on here?"

"We had a little problem, Mr. Thresher," said Robbie.

"I can see that. Exactly what kind of problem, Freddy?"

"Well, umm . . . we were being chased by a swarm of angry bees. We jumped in the lake so they wouldn't sting us."

"A swarm of angry bees? That's scary! Why

was a swarm of angry bees chasing you?" asked my dad.

"Well, ummm . . . it's sort of a long story, Dad," I said, giving Robbie a "help me out here" look.

"We happened to be right under the tree branch when something disturbed the bee's hive, so they chased us, Mr. Thresher."

"Really? Wow! I'm so glad neither one of you got stung. How about if we get in our bathing suits, hang those wet clothes up to dry, and do some fishing?"

"Sounds like a good idea to me," I said cheerfully.

We went back to the campsite, changed into our bathing suits, grabbed our fishing gear, and headed back to the lake.

We found a nice big, flat rock for all of us to sit on. It was right near the water's edge.

"What kind of fish are in this lake, Mr. Thresher?" Robbie asked.

"Trout. I hear they're really big ones, too."

"I'm going to catch the biggest one in the lake," I bragged.

"We'll see about that," said Robbie. "I'm a very good fisherman."

"So, Robbie, you've been fishing before?" my dad asked.

"Oh yeah. Lots of times with my grandpa."

"Well, this is the first time for Freddy and me," my dad said as he tried to hang the lure on the end of the line.

"What's that, Mr. Thresher?" asked Robbie, pointing to the lure.

"If you've been fishing before, then you must know what this is. It's a lure. You know . . . bait for the fish."

"Oh. I've never used one of those."

"You haven't?" I said.

"Nope. Never. My grandpa and I always use worms."

"Worms?"

"Yeah, worms."

"You mean like gummy worms?" I asked.

"No, real, live worms."

"Real, live, ooey, gooey, squishy worms?"

"Yep. You catch the best fish if you use worms."

"Really? Can I try using one?"

"Of course!" Robbie said as he pulled a small jar of worms out of his pocket.

"Hey, where'd you get those?"

"I went digging in my yard early this morning. I found some big, fat, juicy ones. Here," he said, pulling a worm out of the jar. "Try this one. You'll have all the trout in the lake trying to eat that."

He handed me the wriggling worm, and I tried not to let it slip out of my fingers as my dad stuck it on the hook at the end of my fishing line. "Sorry, little guy," I said to the worm, "but you're about to be lunch for a fish!" Then I cast the line out into the water. "Now what?"

"Now you sit and wait," said Robbie. "If you're going to catch a big fish, then you have to be patient."

We sat there quietly for a few minutes, but then I felt a little tug on the end of the line.

"Hey, hey! I think I've got something! I think I've got something!"

"Reel it in! Reel it in!" my dad yelled.

I started to reel in the fish as fast as I could. "I think it's a big one!" I shouted. "He's pulling

pretty hard." I got the fish to the surface of the water. "Look! Look! Do you see him, Dad? Do you see him?" But before my dad could say anything, the fish wiggled free and swam away, and I was left with nothing but an empty hook. "Shoot. He got away," I said, disappointed.

"Here," said Robbie, handing me another worm. "Try again."

"But I'll never catch another fish that big. Did you see him?"

"He was big all right," said my dad. "And I'm sure there are plenty more like him in that lake. But you'll never catch anything unless you put your line back in the water."

I stuck the fresh worm on the hook and threw it back in the lake. Then I waited and waited and waited, but I didn't feel even a single tug on the line.

"Here fishy, fishy, fishy," I called. "Come and get your lunch."

"Ha-ha," Robbie laughed. "They're not dogs, Freddy. They don't come when you call."

"Oh yeah?" I said. "You're wrong—because I've got a huge one tugging on my line right now!" I jumped to my feet so I could use more muscle to reel him in. I planted my feet firmly on the rock and started turning the reel as fast as I could.

"That's it, Freddy!" my dad yelled. "Keep reeling him in. You've almost got him. He's a beaut!"

"Don't worry, Dad. I won't let him get away this time!" I shouted. "Look at him, Robbie! Look!" I screamed as I jumped up and down.

Then, before I knew what was happening, my foot slipped, I lost my balance, and that fish pulled me—*SPLISH, SPLASH*—right into the lake.

"Hey, Freddy. What are you doing?" my dad yelled. "You're supposed to pull the fish out of the lake, not go in after him."

"Ha-ha. Very funny, Dad," I said as he helped pull me out of the water.

"I'm just teasing," said my dad. "Don't get so upset."

"I just can't believe I let that one get away, too. And now I lost the fishing pole. It's somewhere at the bottom of the lake."

"It's not the end of the world."

"But if we don't catch any fish, then what are we going to eat for dinner?"

"I brought along some hot dogs in case the fishing didn't go as well as we planned," my dad said, smiling. "So why don't you and Robbie go for a swim? What do you say?"

I turned to Robbie. "Is that OK with you?"

Robbie smiled, jumped up, and yelled, "Last one in is a rotten egg!" Then he jumped into the lake.

CHAPTER 6

Pass the Marshmallows, Please

After we finished swimming, we walked back to our campsite and put on our clothes. They had dried in the sun.

"I'm starving!" I said. "When's dinner?"

"I figured you boys were probably getting pretty hungry, so as soon as we get our camp-fire going, we can cook the hot dogs."

"And the s'mores," I added.

"Yes, Freddy, and the s'mores," my dad said, smiling. "We just need to pile up some of those sticks you guys gathered earlier today. Where did you put them?"

I looked at Robbie, and Robbie looked at me.

"Yeah. Well, about those sticks . . ."

"What about them?" asked my dad.

"Remember how we were chased by that swarm of angry bees?"

"Yes."

"Well I think we left the sticks on the ground next to that tree when we ran for our lives."

"We could go back and get them, Mr. Thresher," said Robbie.

"That's a great idea. You guys go ahead. I'll stay here and try to get the food organized."

"Are you crazy? I'm not going anywhere near that hive!"

"Don't worry, Freddy," Robbie said. "Those bees aren't there anymore. They flew off some-where else to build another hive."

"Are you sure?"

"What did I tell you earlier?"

"Yeah. Yeah. I know," I said, patting Robbie

on the back. "When it comes to animals, you're the boss. All right. Let's go." We started to walk off. "We'll be back in a few minutes, Dad," I called.

It didn't take us long to reach the big tree. Luckily the bees were gone, but our piles of sticks were still there. We picked them up and ran back to camp.

"Here you go, Dad. Two big piles of firewood."

"Great job, boys. Now let's get this fire started. Whaddya say?"

In no time at all, we had a roaring campfire. "I'm impressed, Mr. Thresher," Robbie said. "This is a great fire you've got here."

"Thanks, Robbie," said my dad. "Your grandpa taught you how to fish, and my grandpa taught me how to build a great fire. He had a house way out in the country, and he had a wood-burning stove to heat his house. Whenever we went to visit, we had to build a fire just to keep warm!"

A growling noise interrupted his story.

"Shhhh. Did you hear that?" Robbie asked. "What was it?"

I burst out laughing. "Ha-ha. Oh, that was just my stomach growling. I think it's saying, 'Time to eat!'"

"Then let's eat!" said my dad. "Here's a hot dog for each of you. Just put it on the end of one of these long sticks and hold it over the fire until the skin cracks a little bit, and it gets hot and juicy."

"You mean I get to cook it myself?" I said excitedly.

"Of course! That's the best part of camping. Cooking out over the campfire. Just don't get too close to the fire."

Soon the hot dogs were done. "Just let them cool a few minutes, and then you can eat them right off the stick," my dad said.

"Really? I wish we could eat like this all the time," I said, blowing on my hot dog to cool it off.

"Yeah," said Robbie. "Who needs silverware?"

I took a bite of my hot dog. "Yum-mm-my!" I said, rubbing my stomach. "I think this is the best hot dog I ever ate."

"Me, too," said Robbie, shoving a huge piece into his mouth.

We gobbled up the hot dogs as if we hadn't eaten in days.

"Time for dessert!" I yelled, and I jumped up and grabbed the bag of marshmallows. "I can already taste the hot, gooey marshmallow melting in my mouth."

"I love s'mores," Robbie said. "Whoever invented them was a genius."

"You can say that again," I said. I stacked three marshmallows on the end of my stick.

"Hey, Freddy, stop being a marshmallow hog, and pass them over here," Robbie said, laughing.

I toasted my marshmallows until they were golden brown. Then I gently slid them off onto a graham cracker, set a piece of chocolate on top, and finished it off with another graham cracker. "Look at that," I said, smacking my lips. "Now *that* is the perfect s'more."

"Are you just going to keep on talking about it, or are you actually going to eat it?" my dad asked.

"Oh, I'm just getting started, Dad. I'm going to eat this one, and then another one, and then another one, and then another one . . ."

"OK, I get the point," he said, chuckling.

We ate s'mores until we couldn't fit another

bite into our stomachs. "I think I'm going to be sick," I said, smiling.

"Well, don't get sick on me," Robbie said. "If you have to toss your cookies, go do it over there," he said, pointing to the bushes.

"I'm just kidding. I'm not really going to throw up."

"Thank goodness," said my dad, "because I'll be in a lot of trouble with your mom if I bring you back sick."

"Actually, I've never felt better," I said, and a big grin spread across my face. "I'm having a great time, Dad."

"Me, too, Mr. Thresher. Thanks for letting me come along."

"My pleasure, Robbie. I'm having a great time, too. Whaddya say we clean up this mess, set up our sleeping bags, and tell some ghost stories?"

"Great idea!" said Robbie. "I have some stories that will really scare the pants off of you!"

CHAPTER 7

Shhhhh,
What's That?

We sat around the campfire for a while telling ghost stories. Actually, Robbie told the stories, and my dad and I listened. I didn't want Robbie to think I was a baby, so I pretended that I wasn't scared even though I was sure some of his stories were going to give me nightmares. Good thing I had found my sharkhead flashlight. I was definitely going to need it tonight.

"Those are some great stories, Robbie," said my dad. "Where did you learn them?"

"Oh, I read them in different books."

Even though Robbie is only in first grade, he is so smart he can read almost anything.

"Didn't you like those stories, Freddy?"

"Uh, yeah. They were . . . uh . . . super. . . ." I said, faking a smile. What I really thought was this: They were super scary.

"I think it's time to put out the campfire and climb into our sleeping bags," my dad said. "We'll just pour some lake water on the fire because we don't want to leave any of it burning overnight. You have to make sure there is not even one ember still burning."

We doused the fire with water and were just about to get into our sleeping bags when I said, "Wait! Wait!"

"What is it, Freddy?"

"I have to go to the bathroom."

"So go."

"Where is it?"

"What do you mean, where is it?"

"I mean, where is the bathroom?"

My dad pointed to the bushes.

"I don't see a bathroom over there."

My dad started laughing.

"What's so funny?"

"Freddy," my dad said, chuckling, "we are out in the wilderness. If you have to go to the bathroom, then you go in the bushes."

"The bushes?!"

"Yep. The bushes."

"But what if some little animal tries to bite me while I'm going to the bathroom?"

Now it was Robbie's turn to laugh. "Ha, ha, ha! Ha, ha, ha! That's hilarious, Freddy." He was laughing so hard he had to hold his sides.

"I'm serious."

"No animal is going to bite you," my dad said. "Just take your flashlight with you and set it on the ground so you can see."

"Are you sure?"

"I'm sure. Now hurry up and go before you have an accident in your pants."

I ran behind the bushes, went to the bathroom as quickly as I ever have in my whole life, and was back in my sleeping bag in a flash.

"Did you even go?" my dad asked.

"Yes, I went. I just went really, really fast."

"Hey, turn off your flashlight, Freddy," said Robbie. "I think I see the Big Dipper."

"Really? Where?" I lay down on my sleeping bag and looked at the stars.

"Right there," Robbie said, pointing up in the sky. "See? It looks sort of like a spoon."

"Oh yeah. I see it now."

"Isn't that the Little Dipper over there?" asked my dad.

"It looks just like the Big Dipper, only smaller," I said.

"Is that why it's called the Little Dipper?" Robbie said, teasing me.

I gave him a playful punch in the arm. "Be quiet."

"Oh, look over there," Robbie continued. "You can see Orion's belt. It looks like a line of three stars in a row."

"Wow! I've never seen so many stars in my

whole life!" I said in amazement. "This is so cool."

"Well I hate to break up the party, but it's time to go to bed now, boys."

"Do we have to, Dad?"

"I'm afraid so. It's getting pretty late, and

you two certainly had a busy day. You must be exhausted. I know I am."

"Come to think of it, I am, too," I said, yawning. "Good night, Dad. Good night, Robbie."

"Good night, Freddy. Good night, Mr. Thresher."

"Good night, boys."

When Robbie and my dad rolled over, I pulled my sleeping bag over my head and secretly turned on my sharkhead flashlight.

Who was I kidding? No matter how tired I was, I was never going to be able to fall asleep out here. I am afraid of the dark at home, and there aren't a lot of strange noises in my bedroom. Out here there was one creepy noise after the next.

I was lying there as still as possible, just listening to the sounds of the night, when all of a sudden, I heard it. *Crunch, crunch, crunch.* It sounded like footsteps on dry leaves.

I lay there frozen in fear. I wanted to reach out to my dad, but I couldn't move a muscle. The footsteps sounded like they were getting closer and closer. *CRUNCH, CRUNCH, CRUNCH.*

My mouth was dry, and my heart was beating a million miles a minute.

CRUNCH, CRUNCH, CRUNCH. The creature was walking right next to my sleeping bag now. I held my breath.

The sound must have woken up my dad because I felt him touch my leg.

"Dad, are you awake?" I managed to say from inside my sleeping bag.

"Yes," he whispered.

"Do you hear that?"

"Yeah. Stay very, very still."

"Why? What is it?"

"A bear."

A bear! Was he kidding?! How could he be so calm?

"He's just looking for some food. He'll be gone in a minute."

Now my heart was beating so hard, I thought it was going to pop out of my chest! A bear! A

bear! A real, live bear just walked right past my sleeping bag!

After what seemed like forever, the sound of the footsteps got quieter as the bear disappeared into the woods. When I couldn't hear them anymore, I poked my dad in the side. "Is he gone?"

"Yes. He's gone."

I peeked out of the sleeping bag. "Just wait till I tell Max Sellars about this. He's never going to believe me! Good thing Robbie was here as my witness."

"I don't think Robbie's going to be much help," my dad said, laughing.

"Why not?"

"See for yourself."

I stuck my head out of my sleeping bag and looked over at Robbie. There he was, all bundled up, snoring away.

My dad and I burst out laughing. "I can't believe he slept through the whole thing!"

CHAPTER 8

P.U., You Stink!

It was a very long night. I didn't get much sleep because I was on the lookout for another bear. Lucky for us, no more bears decided to check out our camp. When the sun finally came up, I was exhausted.

"Hey, Freddy," Robbie said, poking me. "Time to get up."

"UUUGGGHHH!" I groaned.

"What's wrong with you?"

"I'm sooooo tired," I mumbled from inside my sleeping bag.

"Why?"

I stuck my head out of my bag. "Because I was up all night on bear patrol."

"Bear patrol? What are you talking about?"

"Last night a bear walked right past our sleeping bags."

"Ha-ha. Very funny."

"I'm not kidding. You slept through the whole thing!"

"I did?"

"Yep. Look. You can still see his footprints right here in the dirt."

Robbie bent down to examine the dirt more closely. "Wow! You're right. I can see the prints right here."

"I told you so."

"I can't believe I missed the whole thing!"

"Tell me about it. You just went on snoring as if you were in your own bedroom."

"That's crazy," Robbie said, shaking his head in disbelief.

Just then, my dad walked up. "Hey guys, I've got some bad news."

"Can it wait until after breakfast?"

"Nope, because there isn't any breakfast."

"What do you mean?"

"I guess our big furry friend from last night had a craving for doughnuts, and he ate our breakfast as a midnight snack."

"That's OK, Dad. He can have the dough-nuts. I'm just glad he didn't eat us as a midnight snack!"

"We'll stop at a place for breakfast on the ride home. Why don't you boys get your clothes on and your sleeping bags packed up."

"Sure thing, Dad."

We got dressed and packed everything up. While we were waiting for my dad to finish packing the car, we decided to play a game of hide-and-seek.

"Why don't you hide, Robbie, and I'll come look for you," I said.

"OK, Freddy, just give me until the count of fifty to hide."

I covered my eyes and started counting, and
Robbie took off.

"Forty-eight, forty-nine, fifty. Ready or not,
here I come!" I yelled.

I started walking down the path. I looked
behind a big rock, and on the other side of the
tall tree. He wasn't in either of those places. I

was thinking about where to look next when I heard a rustling in the bushes.

"Oh, there you are," I whispered to myself. "You shouldn't have moved. You just gave yourself away."

I tiptoed quietly toward the clump of bushes. I was going to sneak up on Robbie and scare the pants off of him.

When I got really close, I ran around to the

other side of the bushes and yelled, "Boo! I found you!"

To my surprise, it was not Robbie who was hiding in the bushes, but a family of skunks. I must have scared them because before I knew what was happening, the mother skunk lifted her tail and sprayed me.

I turned and ran as fast as I could, scream-ing, "AAAAAHHHHH! Help me! Help me! I've been skunked."

My dad and Robbie came running up the path to meet me, but when they got within inches, they both backed away.

"P.U.," Robbie said, holding his nose and back-ing away even more. "What is that smell?"

"Skunk! I've been skunked!"

My dad and Robbie both started laughing.

"Hey guys, it's not funny."

"I'm sorry, Freddy," said my dad. "You're right. This trip has been a big disaster. You got chased by a swarm of angry bees, you didn't catch any fish, a bear ate your breakfast, and now you got sprayed by a skunk. I guess this was the worst camping trip ever."

"What are you talking about, Dad?" I said, a big grin spreading across my face. "This has been the best camping trip ever!"

And it was.

DEAR READER,

When I was about twelve years old, my class went on a camping trip. We all thought it would be cool to sleep out under the stars, so we didn't put up our tents. In the middle of the night, I heard footsteps, and I woke up just in time to see a big brown bear walk right past my sleeping bag! I have never been so scared in my life. My heart was beating a million times a minute. I will never forget that night.

I hope you have as much fun reading *Camping Catastrophe!* as I had writing it.

HAPPY READING!

Abby Klein

Freddy's Fun Pages

FREDDY'S SHARK JOURNAL

LARGEST, SMALLEST, FASTEST

Sharks live in every ocean of the world.

The largest shark is the whale shark, which can be 46 feet long.

The smallest shark is the dwarf shark, which is 6 to 9 inches long.

The fastest shark is the mako, which can reach speeds of up to 60 miles per hour.

The deadliest animal in the world is the great white shark.

HIDE-AND-SEEK

Can you find the camping words hidden in this word search? Look up, down, across, diagonally, and backward. Good luck!

BEAR   TENT   CAMPFIRE

SKUNK   FLASHLIGHT

BEEHIVE   FISHING   LAKE

TRAIL   BACKPACK

```
S  D  K  Y  K  Z  E  K  S  F

K  T  N  E  T  V  R  C  L  Z

U  R  H  R  I  V  M  A  R  Y

N  F  A  H  W  O  S  P  E  O

K  I  E  Q  B  H  S  K  T  B

L  E  W  A  L  F  J  C  K  E

B  E  R  I  F  P  M  A  C  K

O  F  G  I  R  R  P  B  M  A

O  H  F  I  S  H  I  N  G  L

T  V  V  B  F  D  O  A  D  C
```

FREDDY'S PERFECT S'MORE!

Follow this simple recipe to the make a campfire s'more just like Freddy's. Don't forget to always have the help of an adult.

YOU WILL NEED:

Graham crackers
Marshmallows
Chocolate bars

1. Roast a marshmallow. Freddy likes to roast his on a stick over an open fire.

2. Put the roasted marshmallow on a graham cracker. Be careful! Your marshallow might be very hot.

3. Add a piece of chocolate bar.

4. Put another graham cracker on top.

5. Eat and enjoy!

FUN AROUND THE CAMPFIRE

Here are some of Freddy's favorite camping jokes.

Q. Why don't grizzlies wear shoes?
A. Because they like to walk around in their bear feet!

Q. What do bees use if their hair is messy?
A. A honeycomb!

Q. What fish only swims at night?
A. A starfish!

Q. What's black and white and red all over?
A. A skunk with a diaper rash!

Q. What did the golden retriever take when he went camping?
A. A pup tent!

Q. What are the cleverest bees?
A. Spelling bees!

Q. What do you get if you cross a skunk with a bee?
A. An animal that stinks and stings!

Q. What's the difference between a fish and a piano?
A. You can't tuna fish!

Have you read all about Freddy?

Don't miss any of
Freddy's funny
adventures!